DOUGAL ROUND THE WORLD

'There can be few TV performers who give as much pleasure as Eric Thompson to viewers (or shall we say listeners) of all ages. Long may he and Dougal flourish.'

John Holmstrom in the *New Statesman*

Eric Thompson

DOUGAL
round the world

Based on stories of **The Magic Roundabout** *by Serge Danot*

Illustrated by David Barnett

KNIGHT BOOKS
the paperback division of Brockhampton Press

Also available
THE ADVENTURES OF DOUGAL
DOUGAL'S SCOTTISH HOLIDAY
THE MISADVENTURES OF DOUGAL

ISBN 0 340 16180 9

First published in Great Britain 1972 by Knight Books,
the paperback division of Brockhampton Press Ltd, Leicester

Based on the BBC tv series THE MAGIC ROUNDABOUT

Copyright © 1972 Serge Danot

Illustrations copyright © 1972 Brockhampton Press Ltd

The characters in these stories which appear in the
television films were originally created by Serge Danot for ORTF in a
series entitled *Le Manège Enchanté*, and *The Magic Roundabout*

Printed and bound in Great Britain by
C. Nicholls & Company Ltd, Manchester

CONTENTS

The start

Everyone was sitting in Zebedee's garden. It was a beautiful warm day and no one really felt like doing anything except what they were already doing – sitting in Zebedee's garden. Zebedee wasn't sitting. He was springing in and out of his kitchen serving tea and sandwiches and rock cakes. Dougal sighed, rolled over on to his back and nibbled another cake.

'This is the life,' he said.

'Yes, this is the life,' they all agreed.

Zebedee stopped springing and looked at them all – Dougal lying with his head on a cushion, Brian stretched out on a rug, Dylan fast asleep, Mr Rusty and Mr MacHenry nodding off, and Florence lying with her head resting on Ermintrude.

'More tea anyone?' he said.

Everyone stirred a little.

'I might force down another cup,' said Dougal, lazily.

'And I could toy with another radish butty,' said Brian.

No one else spoke. Zebedee suddenly could stand it no longer.

'WAKE UP!' he shouted.
'ALL WAKE UP!!'
Everyone woke up,
wondering what on earth was the matter.

'What's the matter, Zebedee?' said Florence.

'*You're* the matter,' said Zebedee, 'all of you.
Look at you, lying around doing nothing. I
can't understand why you're all just lying
here! You've all got very lazy lately and I'm
very worried about you.'

'Well, what do you want us to do?' said
Florence.

'I'm not sure,' said Zebedee, 'but I know
you ought to be doing *something*.'

'Would you like me to do a dance?' said Brian, giggling at Dougal.

Dougal giggled back.

'Now you're not being serious,' said Zebedee. 'Listen.'

Everyone put on a serious face and listened.

'I've been thinking,' said Zebedee, 'and I think the time has come for me to take you all in hand. You stay in this garden all day and every day and you never *see* anything else. Your minds will wither – you need to broaden your horizons – you need to get out and about.'

'Perhaps we should go round the world,' said Dougal, 'on a bicycle built for seven.'

Everyone laughed like anything.

'Or we could run,' squeaked Brian. 'Shouldn't take more than fifteen years.'

Everyone shrieked with laughter again.

'Perhaps there's a bus,' said Ermintrude.

This made them laugh even more, and they all rolled about wiping their eyes and choking with mirth.

But Zebedee was looking very thoughtful.

'Um . . .' he said. 'I wonder.'

Gradually they all stopped laughing and looked at Zebedee.

Zebedee looked more thoughtful than ever.

'He's looking a bit thoughtful,' whispered Brian.

Suddenly Zebedee seemed to come to a decision.

'Right,' he said, briskly. 'You've given me an idea. Travel, that's the answer. I don't suppose any of you have ever been *anywhere* or seen *anything*.'

'I've been to London,' said Ermintrude. 'Smithfield. It was great fun.'

'Did you get a prize?' said Florence.

'I'd rather not talk about *that*,' said Ermintrude, darkly.

'Well, I've been to London too,' said Dougal. 'Crufts.'

'Did you get a prize, old pedigree?' said Brian.

'I'd rather not talk about it either,' said Dougal. 'Suffice it to say there was *hanky-panky*.'

Florence was a bit worried. She could see Zebedee was serious.

'Er . . . if we are going to travel,' she asked, 'where are we going?'

'Everywhere,' said Zebedee. 'I'm taking you round the world.'

There was a stunned silence.

'Round the world!' breathed Florence.

'Round the world!' said Dougal.

'Which world does he mean?' said Brian.

'There's only one, you great oaf,' said Dougal. 'You're standing on it.'

'Eek!' said Brian, jumping on to the rug.

Mr MacHenry and Mr Rusty thought they were perhaps a bit old for world travel and they decided to go to Bournemouth instead.

'A spot of sea air,' said Mr Rusty.

'Do us a power of good,' said Mr MacHenry.

So Zebedee agreed that Mr Rusty and Mr MacHenry could go to Bournemouth, but the others were definitely going round the world.

'Willy-nilly?' said Brian.

'Willy-nilly!' said Zebedee.

'Who's this Willy?' said Dougal, furiously.

'No one you know,' said Brian.

Zebedee asked if they were all ready because he was going to start before anything happened to change things.

'I'll take you to Paris first,' he said. 'That's a good place to start round the world from.'

'I can't see it makes much difference,' muttered Dougal.

'Ready?' said Zebedee. 'Close your eyes.'

'Ready,' they all said closing them, and with a magic 'whoosh' they were off, leaving Mr MacHenry and Mr Rusty looking up the train times for Bournemouth. . . .

'You can open your eyes now,' said Zebedee a little later on.

They did so.

'Gracious,' said Florence.

They were all standing on top of a huge tower and all around them, far below, was the city of Paris.

'Paris,'
said Zebedee,
proudly.

'What's this we're standing on?' said Brian.

'The Eiffel Tower,' said Zebedee. 'I chose this because it's high – good for launching.'

'LAUNCHING?!' said Dougal, faintly. 'Launching what?'

'Well, it so happens I have access to a magic carpet,' said Zebedee, 'and you can't beat a magic carpet for actual travel.'

'You don't think we'd do better by BOAC?' said Dougal.

'No, I don't,' said Zebedee. 'Now listen carefully.'

They all listened carefully.

'I have given the instructions,' said Zebedee, 'and I want you all to meet me back in the garden and tell me where you've been. But right round the world, mind – no skipping back when I'm not looking. Right round, mind. Good-bye.'

And with a springing noise he was gone, leaving them all standing on top of the Eiffel Tower feeling a little lost.

'Do you think I've got time to buy a new hat?' said Ermintrude. 'I don't get to Paris often.'

'You're not the only one,' said Dougal.

'May I ask a question?' said Brian.

'No, you may not,' said Dougal.

'Yes, of course you may,' said Florence.

'Oh, once he starts he'll never stop,' said Dougal.

'It's a very *basic* question,' said Brian. 'I just wanted to know where the carpet was.'

Everyone was astounded. No one else had thought of it. Zebedee had gone on and on about the carpet, but no one had thought to ask where it was or how they found it.

'Look,' said Dougal, 'I expect it's all a big joke. Let's go down, get some tea and catch a bus home.'

'No, I don't think it was a joke,' said Florence, slowly. 'Zebedee's not like that.'

She gazed out across the city, shading her eyes with her hand.

'Oo, I think I see something,' she said.

They all looked. Coming towards them was a flat object. It got nearer and nearer, did a zooming turn over the tower and landed just beside them.

It was a carpet, and sitting on it was a little man in a turban and a long robe.

'Afternoon all,' he said, in a broad Lancashire accent. 'You'll be the party then.'

They agreed they probably were the party.

'Thought you might be,' said the man. 'I was told Eiffel Tower. Sorry I'm a bit late, but the thermals were reet tricky over Baghdad. Get on.'

They looked at the carpet doubtfully.

'Is there room for all of us, dear driver?' said Ermintrude.

'The name's Grimbly,' said the little man. 'Mustapha Grimbly, but you can call me George if you've a mind. Ever been on a carpet before?'

They said they hadn't and was it safe?

'Safe as houses,' said George, 'and the best way to travel in the world. I was on the buses before this job. Buses are all right, but you can't beat a carpet.'

He gave a loud laugh.

'Ee . . . that's a good one,' he said, wheezing. 'Can't beat a carpet! Ho! Ho! Ho! What about that?!'

'What about what?' said Dougal.

George looked at him.

'Can't beat a carpet. Don't you get it? Carpet? Beating? Oh, never mind – get on.'

He started to laugh again, muttering 'Can't

15

beat a carpet' to himself.

'We've got a right one here,' whispered Dougal.

They all got on. Although the carpet *seemed* to be quite small there was plenty of room for everyone. George sat at the front, Dougal, Brian and Florence in the middle, and Dylan and Ermintrude at the back.

'Ready?' said George.

'Ready,' they said, a little nervously.

'Right then, we'll be off,' said George, and the carpet rose slowly into the air and set off through the sky across Paris. George took them on a little circular tour so they could have a look round. They saw the churches and the bridges and the river and the stations and the parks.

'No one seems to be taking much notice,' said Florence, looking down.

'It's because we're British,' said Dougal. 'They're like that, the French.'

'Oh,' said Florence.

They flew on over Paris and south across France. It was beautifully warm with just a little breeze and the carpet made no noise at all.

Suddenly Brian gave a great 'whoop!' and started to roar with laughter.

The others looked at him in surprise.

'What's your problem, mollusc?' said Dougal, coldly.

'Can't beat a carpet!' wheezed Brian. 'Oh, that's very good. Hee! Hee! Can't beat a carpet! Ho! Ho! Hee! Hee!'

Dougal sighed.

'What *has* the world done to deserve *him*?' he muttered, and they sped on southwards through the evening sky.

Italy

Everyone was asleep when George landed the carpet on their first stop round the world. The slight bump as they hit the ground woke them up and they all looked around. They were in a beautiful open square. A fountain was splashing and gurgling in the middle and all round there were little cafés with tables and chairs set under big umbrellas.

'Italy,' said George, briefly.

'Oh, I thought Italy was bigger than this,' said Brian.

'Really!' said Dougal. 'Really! This isn't all of it, you great clump. It's twice as big as this *easily*!'

'Where exactly are we, George?' said Florence.

'Florence,' said George.

'Yes?' said Florence.

'Yes,' said George.

'What *are* you two on about?' said Dougal.

'I'm not sure,' said Florence. 'I was just

asking George whereabouts in Italy we were.'

'And I told you,' said George. 'Florence.'

'Yes?' said Florence.

'Yes,' said George, and he began to hoot with laughter.

'Oh dear, he's off again,' whispered Dougal.

'I think he means we're . . . like . . . in the *town* of Florence, mam,' said Dylan.

'Oh,' said Florence. 'He means *Florence*.'

George laughed some more and wiped his eyes.

'Sorry,' he said, 'I never could resist a good jest. Funny, wasn't it?'

'Absolutely hilarious,' said Dougal not laughing at all, but Florence and the others agreed it was a very good joke.

'And I've always wanted to see the Leaning Tower of Florence,' said Brian, happily.

'Oh, you poor befuddled mollusc,' said Dougal, 'don't you know *anything*?'

'Not a lot,' said Brian happily, 'but what I *do* know is very gem-like.'

Dougal groaned.

'Tell him where the Leaning Tower is,' he said to Florence.

'No, *you* tell him,' said Florence, somewhat pointedly.

'Well,' said Dougal, 'it's in . . . it's in . . . um . . . Oh, let him find out for himself.'

'Pisa,' said Ermintrude, suddenly.

'I beg your pardon?' said Dougal.

'Pisa,' said Ermintrude. 'That's where the Leaning Tower is. I remember it from school.'

'Well, I want to see it,' said Brian.

George assured him that they would go and see the Leaning Tower, but first they should all have some breakfast.

'That's the first sensible thing anyone's said for *ages*,' said Dougal, and he led the way across the square to one of the little cafés.

'That was a good joke about Florence, wasn't it?' said Brian, chattily.

'Oh, be quiet,' said Dougal.

After breakfast they wandered round the city and saw all the sights. Ermintrude bought some earrings, Dylan bought a guitar.

'Oh dear,' whispered Dougal, 'now I suppose it's going to be *Tosca* all the way!'

'No,' said Dylan, who had heard, 'but I shall sing to the people and bring . . . like . . happiness into their lives.'

'That's what I was afraid of,' said Dougal, sighing.

'Well, at least he's not asleep,' said Brian.

'You're going to wish he was in a minute,' said Dougal.

Dylan wandered into the middle of a little square and started to play. He was immediately surrounded by dozens of very small children who followed him clapping their hands to the rhythm.

'Rome, Rome for a change,' Dylan sang, and disappeared round a corner surrounded by children.

'There goes the Pied Rabbit of Florence,' giggled Dougal.

George came along and told them they ought to be going if they wanted to see the Leaning Tower before it got dark.

'I'm afraid Dylan's wandered off,' said Florence.

George sighed.

'Aye, someone always wanders off,' he said. 'Never mind. Get on and we'll find him.'

They all got on the carpet and floated over the city looking for Dylan. He wasn't hard to find. He was walking along a wide street followed by about two hundred children all singing at the tops of their voices.

Everyone called to Dylan, but he didn't hear. George swooped low and they shouted again, but still Dylan wandered on, playing and singing.

'I expect he's dropped off,' said Dougal.

'But he's singing,' said Brian.

'That wouldn't stop him sleeping,' said Dougal. 'Not that rabbit.'

George swooped low again and just touched the tips of Dylan's ears. Dylan stopped and looked up.

'Come on!' said Dougal. 'We've got to get to Pisa!'

Dylan climbed on to a low wall, George banked the carpet, flew close to Dylan and the

others pulled him on board.

'Like . . . good-bye, kids!' he shouted, and the children waved and waved until they were just little tiny specks in the far distance.

'Crazy!' said Dylan. 'Really crazy,' and he put down his guitar, curled up and went to sleep.

He was still asleep when they got to Pisa, so they left him while they went to look at the Leaning Tower. George stayed behind too to have a little doze.

The Tower was a marvellous sight, a huge building tilted over at an angle.

'One of the Seven Wonders of the World,' breathed Florence.

'Why is it one of the Seven Wonders?' said Brian.

'Because it's a wonder it doesn't fall over,' said Dougal. 'Anyone can see that.'

'Well, I don't fall over when
I lean,' said Brian, 'so am I a wonder?'

And he stood by the Tower and
leaned as far as he could.

He fell over.

Dougal screeched with laughter.

'You potty little ploppet!' he said.
'Won't you *ever* learn?'

'I hope not,' said Brian.

Ermintrude walked all the way
round the Tower.

'It really is *marvellous*,' she sighed.
'The things you *see* when you travel.'

She yawned and leaned against
the Tower.

It creaked.

'Oh, I feel quite sleepy,' she said,
leaning a bit harder. 'I shall have to
sit down in a minute.'

The Tower creaked again.

'Er . . . Ermintrude . . .,'
said Florence, 'I shouldn't . . .'

But Ermintrude had closed her eyes

and had fallen asleep leaning against
the Tower. As she slept she leaned
harder and harder,
and gradually the Tower got more
and more upright.

'Er . . . Ermintrude,' said Florence
anxiously, 'please wake up.'

The Tower slid a little more.
Ermintrude gave a little snore.
Suddenly the Tower snapped
completely upright, and Ermintrude
slid down and fell over with a bump.

She woke up.

'Oh! It's all right!' she said.
'I was just dozing.'

The others looked at the Tower in
horror.

'Ooh, you've done it now,'
said Dougal.

'Done what, dear dog?'
said Ermintrude.

'You've straightened the Leaning
Tower,' said Florence.

Ermintrude laughed.

'Silly girl,' she said, 'what *do* you mean?'

She turned and looked at the Tower, gave a little 'moo' and fell over in a dead faint.

It was a very difficult moment. Florence flapped her handkerchief at Ermintrude to try to bring her round, Dougal rushed about in little circles and Brian just sat on the ground and laughed.

'What are we going to *do*?' said Dougal, in a frenzy.

'Try pushing it back,' said Brian, giggling.

Florence flapped her handkerchief harder and Ermintrude gradually came to.

'Where am I?' she said, faintly.

'You're very close to the Upright Tower of Pisa,' said Brian.

Ermintrude looked and fainted away again.

'Oh dear, oh dear,' said Florence, 'this really won't do at all. Dougal! Do something!'

'I *am* doing something,' said Dougal. 'I'm circling and *thinking*.'

Florence fanned away at Ermintrude.

'If we could wake her up she might be able to push it over again,' she said.

'We're in a lot of trouble if she can't,' said Dougal. 'People come here to see a Leaning Tower, not an ordinary old upright one.'

'I've got an idea,' said Brian, suddenly.

'Yes?' said Florence.

'Why don't we dig the ground away on one side,' said Brian, 'and then when people stand there one leg will be higher than the other and they'll *lean*.'

'Yes?' said Florence.

'Well, if they lean the Tower will *appear* to lean also,' said Brian, triumphantly.

Dougal stopped circling and looked at Brian.

'Brilliant,' he said. 'Absolutely brilliant. All we need is a couple of bulldozers and about three years hard labour. Great oaf!'

'It was just a thought,' said Brian.

'Well, *stop* thinking if that's the best you can do,' said Dougal.

Suddenly they heard voices.

'Someone's coming,' hissed Dougal. 'Quick! Hide!'

There was nowhere to hide so they all crouched down behind Ermintrude.

The voices got nearer. It was two ladies carrying cameras and talking to each other rather loudly.

'You know I'm sure we should have had a guide, Pauline,' said one.

'Oh, Alice,' said the other, 'what do you

want a guide for? The Leaning
Tower is the Leaning Tower.'

'Oh, what a quaint old seat,'
they said, sitting on Ermintrude
and looking at the Tower.

There was silence for a moment.

'Does that Tower appear to be
leaning to you, Pauline?' said Alice.

'No, Alice, it does not,' said Pauline.
Ermintrude gave a little tiny moo.
'She's waking up!' hissed Brian.
'Well, tell her to stop!' hissed Dougal.
'Stop!' shouted Brian, very loud.
The two ladies jumped into the air.

'I told you we should have had a guide, Pauline,' said Alice nervously, and they both hurried away without looking round.

Ermintrude groaned and stirred. Florence fanned her again and she got up very slowly.

'Thank you, dear heart,' she said. 'Sorry to be a nuisance, but I was quite overcome with shame.'

She looked at the Tower.

'What *have* I done?' she moaned.

'Do you think you could give it a little push back?' said Florence. 'I think it would be best if you could.'

'Well, I'll try, dear, but I feel rather frail at the moment,' said Ermintrude, and she gave the Tower a little push.

It didn't move.

'Try harder,' said Florence.

Ermintrude tried harder. The Tower creaked a little and started to move.

'You're doing it!' shouted Brian. 'Just a bit more!'

Ermintrude pushed a little more. The Tower moved a little more, then a little more and then it started to tilt quite fast.

'You can stop now!' shouted Brian.

'I stopped ages ago,' said Ermintrude.

'Oh lawks!' said Brian.

29

Dougal hurtled round to the other side of the Tower and tried to hold it.

'Come and help!' he screeched.

The Tower tilted dangerously.

'Put a stone under it!' shouted Brian.

'I'll put you under it,' screeched Dougal, but he did manage to push a stone under the bottom.

The Tower gradually stopped.

They stepped back.

'Phew!' said Dougal. 'That was close.'

They looked at the Tower. It was leaning rather more than before. In fact it was leaning a *lot* more than before.

'Do you think anyone will notice?' said Florence, anxiously. 'It's not quite the same as it was.'

'Oh, a leaning tower is a leaning tower,' said Brian. 'I think we did very well.'

'What do you mean, "we"?' said Dougal, panting.

'Well, I encouraged by my presence and my cool thinking,' said Brian. 'They also serve who only stand and watch, you know.'

'And they also get thumped who only talk too much,' said Dougal, threateningly.

'Don't you dare!' said Brian. 'I'm littler than you.'

'Now stop that, you two,' said Florence. 'I'm sorry to have been a nuisance,' said Ermintrude.

'That's all right,' said Florence.

They went back to the carpet. George was busy making sandwiches and opening bottles of milk.

'Seen enough?' he asked.

'For a lifetime,' said Dougal, with feeling.

They all had something to eat. Dylan woke up and joined them.

'Have I got . . . like . . . time for a quick peep at the Tower?' he said.

'If you're very quick,' said George, and Dylan went to have a look while the others cleared up.

'That's the craziest thing,' said Dylan when he came back.

31

'How does it ever stay
leaning like that
without falling over?'
'It's got a stone under it,'
said Brian.
'And I hope no one ever
moves it,' muttered Dougal.
'Right, ready to go?'
asked George.
Everyone got on the carpet.
'Where are we going now?'
asked Florence.
'You're all going to sleep,'
said George, 'and when you wake up
you'll see. Reet?'
'Reet,' they said, and they floated
up over Pisa, did a turn round the Tower
with George looking at it in rather a
puzzled way, and headed south again
through the warm evening air.

Morocco

Everyone was asleep when they landed again.
The little bump woke them up, and they all
yawned and stretched and looked around.
George had brought the carpet down close to
a little clump of palm-trees and all around as
far as the eye could see there was nothing but
sand.

'I think the tide's out,' said Brian, brightly.
'Must be Clacton.'

'Oh, don't be such a great oaf,' said Dougal.
'It's nothing like Clacton.'

'Have you ever been to Clacton?' said
Brian.

'That's beside the point,' said Dougal.

'No, it's beside the *sea*,' said Brian.

Florence told them to stop arguing and asked George if there was anywhere close they could go for breakfast.

'All taken care of,' said George. 'All part of the service,' and he gave a piercing whistle. A large clump of dates dropped out of the palm-tree, landed on Dougal's head and finished up in the centre of the carpet

George looked up.

'Funny,' he said, 'that's never happened before. Anyway, try some of those to be going on with,' and he gave another very loud whistle.

Dougal winced.

'I hope he doesn't do that often,' he said. 'I've got very sensitive ears.'

Ermintrude was munching a date.

'Ooh, delicious,' she said. 'Do try some.'

They all tried some and admitted they were indeed very delicious.

'There's nothing like a date fresh from the palm,' sighed Ermintrude.

'And there's nothing like tea fresh from the pot,' said Dougal, 'but I suppose I shall have to wait till I get home for *that*.'

He was wrong. A small cloud of dust appeared on the horizon. Something was coming towards them very fast. It got nearer and nearer and finally stopped. The dust settled slowly and there was a camel with a basket hanging on either side of its hump.

'Sorry to be late, George,' it said. 'Terrible crowd in Marrakesh.'

'That's all right, Sandy,' said George, 'we've only been here a minute.'

He went across to the camel and started to get things out of the baskets. There was a table-cloth, knives, forks and spoons, teacups and saucers, plates and bowls, a large pot of tea, milk and sugar, lettuce and cucumber, cornflakes and boiled eggs.

'Well!' said Ermintrude. 'We can hardly complain about the service.'

'No, we certainly can't,' said Florence, happily. 'I like going round the world.'

They all had breakfast and when they had finished George packed the things back in the baskets.

'What's the plan then, Sandy?' he asked.

The camel munched a date thoughtfully.

'Well,' he said, 'I thought they'd like a quick saunter round the market now, flip over the Atlas Mountains for a cup of coffee, drop in at Casablanca for lunch, tea at Joe's Oasis Caff and early bed in Fez. What do you think?'

He got up and sauntered over to Ermintrude.

'How about you and me taking a quick look

at the Casbah?' he said, with a huge wink.

'Cheeky thing,' said Ermintrude, giggling.

'Don't take any notice of him, miss,' said George, 'he's quite harmless.'

Ermintrude looked a little disappointed, the camel munched another date, gave another big wink and went back to George.

'Well?' he said.

'Fine,' said George, 'we'll do what you say. Carpet or train?'

'Well, carpet's quicker, but train is more interesting,' said Sandy.

'What *are* they talking about?' hissed Dougal. 'How do we get a train out here?'

'I think they probably know what they're talking about,' said Florence, but she did see Dougal's point – there didn't seem much chance of catching a train from where they were. There wasn't even a station.

But George let out another of his piercing whistles and in the distance another cloud of dust appeared.

'Train's coming,' said George, briefly.

'Good-bye, all,' said Sandy, and he trotted away just as the other cloud of dust arrived.

It was six camels.

'All aboard,' said George, and he folded the carpet neatly, asked the first camel to kneel down and threw the carpet across its neck.

'All aboard,' he said again.

'This is a *train*?' said Dylan.

'Camel train,' said George. 'Hurry up.'

The camels all knelt down and waited.

'Which bit do you sit on?' whispered
Florence.

'Don't ask me,' whispered Dougal.

They watched George as he got on his
camel. He gave a little jump and sat on top of
the hump.

'Come on,' he said, 'or we'll never get
there.'

'I'm not sure we'll get there anyway,'
muttered Dougal, but he got on a hump and
perched there wobbling.

'Dougal of Arabia, I presume?' said Brian.

'I'll throw a clump of dates at you if you're
not careful,' said Dougal. 'Just get on and be
quiet.'

So Brian got on and so did Florence and
Dylan. Ermintrude had a little difficulty.

'I think someone will have to give me a leg
up,' she wailed.

George got off and went over to
Ermintrude. He looked at her and he looked
at the camel.

'Everybody come and help,' he said, 'this

might be difficult.'

Everyone got off again and went over to help Ermintrude.

'Now when I say "push", push,' said George.

'PUSH!'

Everyone pushed. Ermintrude slithered up the side of the camel, teetered for a moment on the top and then slithered down the other side with a bump. They tried again. Ermintrude went up again, teetered again and slid off again.

'Try holding on,' said Florence.

'What *with*, dear thing?' said Ermintrude.

They pushed again, and again she fell off.

Ermintrude was furious and became very determined.

'Stand aside!' she ordered, and strode off into the desert.

'Where's she going?' said Brian.

'I can't imagine,' said Dougal.

Ermintrude stopped about fifty yards away. She turned, lowered her head, gave a little moo, thundered towards the camel and leapt on.

'I'm on!' she cried. 'I'm on! Let's go! What are we all waiting for?!'

The others got back on and waited for George to start.

'Hold on,' he said. 'Here we go.'

The camels got up on to their back legs. Everyone slithered forward. Then the camels got on to their front legs. Everyone slithered back again.

Ermintrude fell off.

'Oh, this is the last straw!' she wailed.

The camel turned his head slowly.

'You may be right, madam,' he said, laconically.

This made Ermintrude more determined than ever. She rushed at the camel and leapt on again. This time she stayed on.

'Bravo!' everyone shouted, and they were off in a single file across the desert.

It was a very strange sight. George leading and singing 'She's a lassie from Lancashire'; Florence next, perched high on her camel and singing the choruses with George; then Dylan, fast asleep, having tied himself on with a rope; then Brian, who had retired into his shell and was looking rather like a hump on top of a hump; then Dougal, who had slithered off the camel's back on to its neck and was clinging on grimly; and last Ermintrude, happily astride and giving an occasional moo of delight.

They approached a huge red wall. Behind it they could see towers and palm-trees, and they could hear a lot of noise.

George turned and shouted over his shoulder.

'Market!'

They went through a low gate in the wall and found themselves in a huge open square. It was crowded with people and very noisy. George led the way and finally stopped under some palm-trees by a little pool of water. The camels knelt down and everyone fell off except Dylan who was still tied on and still asleep.

Dougal looked at him.

'He'll set the record for round-the-world sleeping, that rabbit,' he said, untying the rope.

Dylan fell off.

'What? Like . . . er . . . what?' he said. 'Where are we, man? Like . . . where?'

'It's Notting Hill Gate,' said Dougal, sarcastically.

'Oh,' said Dylan, and he rolled over and went back to sleep.

George gave the camels some dates and told them they'd be back soon.

'I expect you'd all like a little something?' he said to the others.

'I should love a little something,' said Brian. 'Is there an Arabian radish?'

'I shouldn't wonder,' said George. 'Come along, all.'

They started to go, but Florence noticed Ermintrude wasn't with them.

'Where's Ermintrude?' she said.

They looked. There was no sign of her.

'Perhaps she sneaked off for a hay sandwich,' said Dougal. 'Be just like her.'

'We'd better find her,' said Florence, anxiously.

'Aye, we'd better,' said George.

So they set out to look for Ermintrude.

They went through the market-place and looked amongst all the people. No Ermintrude. They asked a group of donkeys if they'd seen her, but they hadn't. They asked a tall Arab policeman, but he hadn't seen her either. They wandered in and out of the market stalls, past jugglers and fortune-tellers, past fruit-stands and sweet-stands, but there was no sign of Ermintrude anywhere.

Finally, they came to a café and all sat down, feeling rather tired. Brian and Florence ordered some orange juice and Dougal and George ordered some tea. The waiter brought it. The orange juice looked just like orange juice, but the tea was in a tall glass full of green leaves.

'What's this!?' said Dougal.

'That's tea,' said George.

'TEA!!' said Dougal. 'It looks like a glass of wet grass!!'

'It's mint tea,' said George. 'Very refreshing.'

Dougal looked at the glass of mint tea.

'Oh, to be in England,' he sighed, and took a sip.

It was very sweet and very good.

'Ooh!' he said, brightening. 'Not bad.'

'There you are, Dougal,' said Florence. 'You must always be prepared to try something *new*.'

'Want some?' said Dougal.

'No, thank you,' said Florence.

They gazed around. The square was full of colours and the sun was very hot. The only thing missing was Ermintrude.

Yoo! Hoo! Yoo! Hoo! they heard.

'That's Ermintrude!' said Florence.

Yoo! Hoo! Yoo! Hoo! they heard again, and Ermintrude appeared followed by a very small Arab in a very large robe.

She sat down.

She was wearing a veil over her face, a huge pair of bloomers covered in a violent flower design and had a large handbag hanging round her neck.

'I've been shopping,' she said, happily.

'We'd never have known,' said Dougal, giggling.

'What's that on your face?' said Brian,
hanging on to his chair and laughing.

'It's my yashmak,' said Ermintrude,
proudly. 'No lady wanders about *here* without one.'

Dougal and Brian clung on to each other,
laughing like anything.

'Who's your friend?' they hooted, pointing
to the small Arab in the robe.

'This is Mustapha,' said Ermintrude. 'He's
been *very* helpful.'

Mustapha pointed at Ermintrude.

''Ow much?' he said.

George shook his head.

'Not for sale,' he said.

Mustapha looked surprised.

''Ow much?' he said again.

45

'Poor boy,' said Ermintrude, 'I think he wants to buy me.'

'How much will you give us!?' shouted Brian and Dougal, but Florence told them not to be silly.

'I'm afraid our friend is not for sale,' she said to Mustapha.

'Yours for four pence!!' screeched Dougal and Brian, purple with mirth.

'Now hush, you two!' said Florence, and she told Ermintrude not to wander off by herself in future.

'Sorry, dear thing,' said Ermintrude. 'Good-bye, Mustapha dear!'

Mustapha bowed and started to go away. Then he came back and pointed at Brian.

''Ow much?' he said.

'Nothing!' shouted Dougal. 'Take him! A present!'

'Don't be rotten!' said Brian, clinging on to his chair and squeaking.

Mustapha bowed again, looked round and then wandered away.

'Nearly got rid of you that time!' said Dougal.

'Didn't want to buy *you* though, did he?' jeered Brian.

'Now once and for all stop it, you two,' said Florence, severely.

So Brian and Dougal stopped it and they all
followed George back to the camels.

'I think we'll take the carpet now,' said
George. 'Thanks, lads.'

They all thanked the camels for the ride
across the desert. Then they woke Dylan up.

'Time to go,' they said.

'Already?' said Dylan, stretching. 'It's a
great place this.'

'You know,' whispered Dougal, 'I think he
may get round the world without seeing
anything but the ground he's lying on.'

'Well, he's enjoying himself,' whispered
Brian. 'That's the main thing.'

And that did seem to be the main thing as
they got on the carpet, rose high over the
market square and flew eastwards away from
the setting sun.

India

The first thing they noticed when they landed again was the heat. It was very hot even though it was early in the morning.

'Where are we?' said Florence.

'India,' said George. 'Great little place. I always like coming here.'

'Isn't this where all the tea comes from?' said Dougal, thoughtfully.

'A lot of it,' said George. 'Do you want some?'

Dougal said he would rather like some, so they all had breakfast brought on trays by Indians in very bright coloured turbans.

After breakfast they took a little walk. For

some reason Ermintrude was a great favourite
wherever they went. People hung flowers
round her neck, great garlands of yellow and
white and red. She looked very pretty.

'You look very pretty, Ermintrude,' said
Florence.

'Thank you, dear,' said Ermintrude, as
another string of flowers was added by yet
another admirer.

'She won't be able to see soon,' whispered
Dougal.

'She is a bit festooned,' whispered Brian.

They came to a large open square and
stopped to look around.

49

'Want to see some snake-charmers?' asked George.

'Oo, yes please,' said Florence.

'Er . . . just a moment,' said Dougal. 'Did you say *snake*-charmers?'

'Yes,' said George. 'Snakes. Cobras, adders, things like that.'

'Actual *poisonous* snakes?' said Dougal.

'So they tell me,' said George. 'Don't you like them?'

'Oh no, it's not *that*,' said Dougal. 'I mean, some of my best friends . . . er . . . but . . .'

'Oh, come on, old charmer,' said Brian. 'Let's go and have a look.'

'I'm *coming*,' said Dougal. 'Don't rush me!'

They went into the middle of the square. Sitting on the ground was an old man in a loin-cloth and a turban. He had a pipe-like instrument in his hands and a basket at his feet. George greeted him and whispered something in his ear.

The man nodded, gave a little cough and started to play the pipe. The music was very weird.

'Oh, that's beautiful,' said Dylan, closing his eyes. '*Beautiful*,' and he sat down and nodded off to sleep.

The music continued.

'Where are the snakes?' hissed Dougal.

'Is that one behind you?' said Brian.

Dougal gave a screech and leapt three feet into the air.

'Oh no, sorry,' said Brian, 'it's just a twig.'

'Oo!! One of these days . . . !' said Dougal, threateningly.

'Sh!!' said Florence. 'Something's happening.'

Something was.

Out of the basket came a cobra, waving and weaving to and fro. The music got louder and faster, and more and more of the cobra appeared. Its hood was spread wide and it looked rather dark and sinister. Then it slithered out of the basket completely and sat on the ground with its head in the air.

The music stopped. The snake turned and looked at them with little glittering eyes.

'I think he's got his eye on you,' said Brian.

Dougal backed away behind Ermintrude.

'Very interesting,' he said.

The Indian looked at them and held the pipe out in his hand.

'He wants to know if anyone would like to have a go,' said George.

'Go on, Dougal!' said Florence.

'Yes, go on, Dougal!' they all said.

'Who, me?' said Dougal. 'Not likely!'

'Go on,' they shouted, 'don't be a spoil-sport.'

'I'm not spoiling anyone's sport,' said Dougal. 'You have a go, if you're so keen.'

'I don't think ladies are allowed to,' said Florence.

'And I'm too small,' said Brian.

'And Dylan's asleep,' said Ermintrude.

'So that leaves *you*,' they said.

They pushed Dougal forward. He went very reluctantly.

'All right! All right! Don't push!' he said.

The Indian gave him the pipe. Dougal looked at the cobra nervously. He gave a little toot. The cobra stayed quite still. Dougal gave another little toot and then blew very hard as the cobra came a little way towards him. The music Dougal played was quite unearthly, but the cobra raised itself and swayed to and fro.

It came a little closer to Dougal.

'If you think that's charming I've got news for you,' it hissed.

Dougal stopped playing.

'I'm doing my best,' he whispered. 'I'm not used to this, you know.'

'Well, don't blow so hard,' said the cobra, 'and we'll all enjoy ourselves more.'

Dougal played less hard. The cobra swayed and slithered.

'That's much better, boyo,' it said, and when Dougal gave a final little toot it disappeared into the basket.

Everyone applauded.

'You were wonderful, Dougal,' said Florence. 'I didn't know you could charm snakes.'

'Neither did he,' said Brian, quietly.

'What?!' said Dougal.

'Nothing,' said Brian.

They thanked the snake-charmer, woke Dylan up and went on. In another part of the square there was a large crowd. They went across to have a look. Another Indian in a turban was playing a pipe and in front of him was another basket.

'Another snake-charmer?' said Florence.

'Just watch,' said George.

The Indian played his pipe, and as he did so a small boy started to twirl and dance in front of him. He twirled and twirled and leapt and leapt. Finally he put his hand into the basket and pulled out – a long coil of rope.

'That's a funny looking snake,' said Dougal.

'Just watch,' said George.

The pipe played and the boy whirled some more, this time twirling the coil of rope round and round. Then he threw one end of it into the air with a great shout and stood quite still. The pipe stopped playing. There was silence.

The rope didn't fall back to the ground.

It stayed stretched up into the air even though there was nothing to hold it. It was as though someone had attached it to a hook in the sky.

'Gracious,' said Florence.

'Just watch,' said George.

The pipe started to play again, and the small boy took hold of the rope and pulled. It stayed where it was. The pipe played some more and the boy began to climb the rope. Up and up he went, right to the top; then he gave a great shout, the pipe stopped playing, the rope fell to the ground and the boy landed on his feet beside it.

Everyone applauded and cheered like anything.

'I don't believe it,' breathed Florence.

'No, not many people do,' said George.

'I want to have a go! I want to have a go!' said Brian. 'I want to have a go at the rope trick!'

Everyone laughed and laughed, but Brian was allowed to have a go.

'Can my friend play the pipe?' he asked.

The Indian nodded and handed the pipe to Dougal.

'You'll never do it,' he said to Brian. 'Stop being such a great clump.'

'Just play,' said Brian. 'We snails are very deft in our own way.'

Dougal sighed and started to play the pipe. Brian whirled and whirled, squeaking with delight. He disappeared into his shell.

'Sorry,' he said, coming out again. 'I didn't mean to do that.'

'Oh, get on with it,' said Dougal.

Brian whirled some more, got hold of the rope in his mouth and with a great squeak threw it into the air. It went up and up, and then came down again and coiled itself over Brian, covering him completely.

Dougal nearly swallowed
the pipe with laughter.

'Why's it gone dark?' said
Brian, in a muffled voice.

Florence uncoiled the rope
from Brian.

'I don't think you got it quite
right,' she said.

Brian looked at Dougal suspiciously.

'Were you playing the right tune?'
he asked.

'How should I know?' said Dougal.

'Well, try again,' said Brian.

They tried again. Dougal blew and blew,
and Brian threw the rope up again with a
shout.

It stayed there. It was not quite straight.
In fact it looked a bit like steps made of rope,
but it stayed there.

'I've done it!' shouted Brian, and he started
to go up the steps.

'Careful, Brian!' called Florence.

Brian reached the top and stood there.

Everyone applauded and cheered. Brian gave a great shout of triumph – and disappeared.

There was silence.

'He's disappeared!' whispered Florence.

The crowd began to murmur in wonderment.

Ermintrude went over to the rope and looked up.

'He's certainly not there,' she said. 'Wherever can he have got to?'

'Try playing a tune, Dougal,' said Florence.

Dougal sat in silence looking up at the rope.

'Dougal!' said Florence again. 'Try a little tune.'

Dougal didn't seem to hear. A tear rolled down his face.

'My little chum,' he sniffed. 'Gone, and never even said good-bye. I should never have let him try it. I'm a beast!'

And he burst into tears and buried his head in the basket.

'Now, Dougal,' said Florence, 'this isn't being any help at all.'

'He didn't even take a lettuce with him,' wailed Dougal. 'He'll get hungry!'

And he buried his head in the basket again.

'Dougal!' said Florence. 'Pull yourself together.'

Dougal wailed louder than ever.

'My little perky friend,' he moaned, 'he's left me all alone.'

'Not quite alone, dear thing,' murmured Ermintrude. '*We're* here.'

'It's not the same,' howled Dougal, and buried his head in the basket again as Brian popped his head out of it.

'Evening all!' he said, laughing.

'Brian!!' said Florence, hugging him. 'We thought we'd lost you.'

'Oh, you did give us a turn, you naughty thing!' said Ermintrude.

'Sorry,' said Brian.

He turned to Dougal.

'Hallo,' he said.

Dougal looked at him for a long moment.

'Snail,' he said, 'I'll give you a count of three to get out of that basket and out of my sight, you great blundering disappearing OAF, YOU!!!! ONE!'

Brian got out of the basket.

'Did you miss me?' he said.

'TWO!' said Dougal, threateningly.

'Why's your face all red?' said Brian.

'THREE!' said Dougal, and he leapt at Brian and chased him into the crowd.

Everyone cheered and hooted.

'You know, I think they're quite fond of each other really,' said Ermintrude.

'Of course they are,' said Florence, 'but I wonder how Brian did that trick?'

There was a 'bong' and Zebedee landed beside her.

'Zebedee!' said Florence. 'I might have known!'

'Just dropped in to see how you were getting on,' said Zebedee. 'Everything going all right?'

'We're having a wonderful time,' said Florence.

There was a screech and Brian hurtled back into the square followed by Dougal.

'Stop it, you two,' said Florence, 'Zebedee's here.'

Dougal slithered to a halt in a cloud of dust and looked at Zebedee.

'Ah! I might have known,' he said. 'It was *you*, wasn't it?'

'I like to keep my hand in,' said Zebedee, 'and it's a long time since I made a snail disappear up a rope.'

'No, not something one does every day,' said Ermintrude, thoughtfully.

'Well, I wish you'd do it again,' grumped Dougal.

'Now, Dougal,' said Florence, 'you know you don't mean that.'

'You don't mean it! You don't mean it!' shouted Brian.

Dougal sat on him.

'Having good weather back home?' he said to Zebedee, chattily.

'Tolerably,' said Zebedee, 'thank you. Which reminds me, I must be off again. Glad you're having a good time.'

And he bonged away.

'Now, Dougal,' said Florence, 'get up off Brian and come along. It's time to go.'

Dougal got up. 'Oh, hallo!' he said to Brian. 'I didn't see you there.'

'I shall forgive you,' said Brian slowly, 'because I am high-minded and lovable, but there are times when you go too far.'

'Oh, come on,' said Dougal, 'or we'll miss the carpet and I don't want to be stuck in India with *you*.'

They all got back on to the carpet and rose into the air again, waving good-bye to everyone left in the square.

'Now which way shall we go?' muttered George to himself. 'Which way?'

A huge bird flapped slowly along beside them. It was a vulture.

'What's the traffic like over Burma, Elsie?' shouted George.

'Oh, my dear,' said the vulture, 'you know what Burma's like this time of the year.'

'Bad?' said George.

'Like Southend on August Bank Holiday,' said Elsie.

'Thank you,' said George.

'You're welcome,' said Elsie, and she flapped slowly away.

'We'll go the long way round,' said George. 'Elsie always knows,' and he turned the carpet and flew northwards.

'What *I* want to know,' said Dougal darkly, 'is how a vulture from India knows about Southend.'

'I expect she pops over there for a piece of rock,' said Brian.

'You'll get a piece of rock if you're not careful,' said Dougal. 'Right on the bonce.'

'Dougal, don't be vulgar,' said Florence.

She looked down. They were flying over some very high mountains covered in snow.

'Oh, how beautiful,' she breathed. 'Look!'

They looked.

'Himalayas,' said George, briefly. 'Mount Everest on the left.'

He looked down and waved. Away in the distance, almost on top of the highest mountain in the world, was a furry figure. It waved back.

'Friend of yours?' they said.

'Sort of,' said George.

'What's his name?' they said.

'Yeti,' said George, and he turned the carpet northwards, leaving the mountains far behind.

North Pole

When they woke up again they were in what seemed to be a very strange place. The light was very bright and white, and there was nothing but snow and ice as far as the eye could see.

George was sitting on the front of the carpet wrapped in a huge padded jacket with just the tip of his nose showing.

'You'll need your parkas,' he said, pointing to a huge pile of grey clothes.

Everyone put on a parka. They were all like the one George was wearing – padded and warm and with hoods to put over the head. Brian's was a bit like a sleeping bag so he got inside.

'Will someone pull it tight round my neck?' he asked.

'With pleasure,' said Dougal, and he pulled with his teeth at the cord round Brian's neck.

'Eeek!' said Brian, going purple. 'Not so tight!!'

'Sorry,' said Dougal, fiendishly.

Ermintrude slung her parka over her back and popped the hood over her head.

'I don't really feel the cold,' she said, 'but I suppose it's as well to be *prepared*.'

George said they would go and have some breakfast when they were all ready.

'I've got some transport laid on,' he said.

'Can't we take the carpet?' said Florence.

'No anti-freeze,' said George briefly, 'but I'll be here when you get back.'

'Oh, right,' they said.

'Here it comes,' said George, and across the ice came a large sledge pulled by seven huge dogs.

Dougal went quite pale.

'I say,' he said faintly, 'I hope you don't expect *me* to do that, do you?'

The sledge came to a halt in a flurry of snow and six of the dogs lay down on the ice, panting. The seventh, and biggest, came across to the group.

'Hallo, Pixie,' said George.

'*Pixie!!?*' hissed Dougal.

The sledge-dog growled hallo at George and came across to Dougal.

'So you're the new boy, eh?' he snarled, showing a great many teeth.

'Well . . . er . . . not exactly,' said Dougal. 'I mean . . . I . . . er . . .'

'I was told there was a sledge-dog here, so I only brought six of the boys,' said Pixie. 'Union rules calls for eight. So are you or aren't you?'

'Oh yes, he is!' squeaked Brian. 'He's been looking forward to it!'

'Be quiet!' hissed Dougal.

Pixie went back to George.

'Got a bit of trouble here,' he said. 'Can't move without eight dogs.'

'He says he can't move without eight dogs,' called George.

'Well, he moved here with *seven*,' shouted Dougal.

'Special circumstances,' growled Pixie.

'Special circumstances!' shouted George.

Dougal groaned.

'I think I can see how this is all going to end up,' he said.

'Do it for us, Dougal,' said Florence.

'Oh, wheedle, wheedle!' muttered Dougal.

'Think of the experience,' said Brian.

'I *am* thinking,' said Dougal, 'and that's just the trouble.'

'Think of *breakfast*, Dougal,' said Florence.

Dougal groaned again.

'Oh, all right!' he said. 'What do I do?'

Everyone got on the sledge while Pixie harnessed Dougal to a long line. All the other dogs looked at Dougal with interest.

'When I say "MUSH", you pull,' said Pixie.

'MUSH!?' said Dougal. 'Is that absolutely necessary?'

'Union rules,' said Pixie.

He went to the end of the line, winking at the other dogs. They all nodded back.

Dougal turned.

'Keep your eyes strictly to the front!' snarled Pixie.

'I know! I know! Union rules!' muttered Dougal, fixing his eyes firmly to the front.

'MUSH!' barked Pixie, and Dougal pulled. As he did so the other dogs quietly stood to one side and as Dougal hauled at the sledge they all got on, winking at each other.

'MUSH! MUSH!' shouted Pixie, and Dougal pulled and pulled.

On board there were great hissings and splutterings of laughter.

'We always do this to someone new,' giggled one.

'It's a trick we have,' they hooted.

On the end of the long line Dougal pulled and panted.

'Union rules,' he grumbled. 'Huh!'

They came to a large log cabin.

'Whoa!!' shouted Pixie, and Dougal stopped thankfully.

'You can turn round now,' they shouted, and Dougal turned and looked. Everyone was sitting on the sledge laughing like anything.

Dougal looked at them.

'I suppose you think that's very funny,' he said.

'Are you very tired, Dougal?' said Florence, anxiously.

'Oh, no!' said Dougal, sarcastically. 'I've just pulled about fourteen tons of dead weight a hundred miles across the ice – why should I be tired?'

Florence put her arm round him.

'Come and have some breakfast,' she said. 'I'm sorry they played a trick on you.'

'I quite enjoyed it actually,' said Dougal.

So they went to have some breakfast, leaving Pixie and the others hooting with laughter in the snow.

'Uncouth lot,' muttered Dougal with dignity.

Inside the hut breakfast was being prepared by some creatures completely covered in white fur. One, the biggest, was at a large stove cooking something. Another, not quite so big, was laying the table, and a third, quite small, was setting out chairs. They were polar bears.

'Porridge?' said the biggest one.

'Er . . . that would be lovely,' said Florence, nervously.

'Kindly sit down then,' said the middle-sized one.

'Not there!' shouted the little one, just as Dougal was about to sit down.

Dougal leapt up.

'That's my chair!' said the little one.

'Sorry,' muttered Dougal, sitting somewhere else.

'*You* can sit in my chair,' said the little one to Florence.

'Thank you,' murmured Florence, sitting.

'It's just that we did have some trouble once before,' whispered the middle-sized bear, 'and he's never forgotten it.'

Ermintrude sat in the biggest chair and it collapsed under her with a crash.

The biggest bear turned slowly at the stove.

'It's happened again, Mother,' he said.

'I'm afraid it has, Father,'
was the reply.

'I'm very sorry,'
said Ermintrude, faintly.

'That's all right,'
sighed the bears.

Everyone had some porridge, and when
they had finished they thanked the bears and
went outside.

Pixie and the others were waiting.

'Want to go to the North Pole?' they said.

'Not if I've got to pull,' said Dougal, grimly.

'Not this time,' they assured him and
everyone, including Dougal, sat on the sledge
while Pixie and the others harnessed
themselves up.

'You know, mam, those bears remind me of
something,' Dylan said to Florence.

'I was just thinking the same thing,' said Florence.

'Good porridge though, wasn't it?' said Brian, happily.

'Too hot,' growled Dougal, and they were off, travelling very fast across the ice with Pixie in the lead and Brian standing on the front of the sledge shouting 'MUSH' with all his might.

They came to a halt after a while and the dogs lay down on the ice, panting.

'Here we are,' said Pixie.

They all looked around. There was nothing to be seen.

'Here we are, where?' said Brian.

'North Pole,' said Pixie.

'I can't see an Eskimo, let alone a Pole,' giggled Dougal.

'I think there should be a Pole of some sort, said Ermintrude, 'otherwise it doesn't seem quite fair to anyone who's come all this way.'

'Well, it's always been like this,' said Pixie.

Ermintrude looked at him.

'I can see no reason why that means it should *stay* like this,' she said, 'and I, for one, intend to do something about it.'

'What had you in mind, Ermintrude?' said Florence.

72

'Well, I thought something fairly tasteful in the *flag* line,' said Ermintrude. 'Perhaps one marked "With love from Ermy".'

'That's *tasteful*?' whispered Brian.

'Oh, leave her alone,' said Dougal. 'She'll never find a flag here anyway.'

But Ermintrude had brought her handbag with her and she began to rummage through it.

'Funny,' she muttered, 'I usually have a flag or two with me, just in case. Ah!'

She pulled out of her handbag the enormous pair of bloomers she had bought in Morocco.

'*Just* the thing,' she mooed. 'Now no one will be able to mistake the place. Pixie dear, have you got a pole?'

Pixie growled and had a look on the sledge.

'There's a fishing rod,' he said.

'That will do perfectly,' said Ermintrude, and she made a hole in the ice, stuck the fishing rod in and fastened the bloomers to the top. They made a brave show but were soon frozen stiff.

'It'll be a bold explorer who thaws *those* out,' said Dougal, and he and Brian giggled away as Ermintrude saluted her new flag and got back on the sledge.

'Come along,' she said. 'Let's go and see something else.'

'Ermintrude, you're wonderful,' said Florence.

'I know, dear,' said Ermintrude, and they went off to see something else.

Pixie and the others pulled them across the ice.

'Where do you want to go?' they called.

'Anywhere you like,' shouted Florence, so they went on until they came to a low, round building.

'What's *this*?' said Dougal.

'Igloo,' said Brian.

'I beg your pardon?' said Dougal.

'Igloo,' said Brian. 'It's an igloo – that's what it's called, an igloo. Igloo . . . ig . . .'

'All right, all right!' said Dougal. 'I think we have the general idea.'

They all got off the sledge and went across to the igloo. There was a little notice on the outside.

'BIG JANE'S PLACE' it said. 'ALL WEL-COME. ICE-CREAM A SPECIALITY.'

And just underneath was an arrow pointing straight down.

'Where's the door?' said Dougal.

'I suppose that arrow is pointing to it,' said Dylan, yawning.

'Just woken up?' said Dougal.

'Like . . . this minute,' nodded Dylan.

Brian gave a little squeak.

'In here!' he said, and they looked just in time to see Brian disappearing into a little icy tunnel. Dougal peered into it.

'He's gone!' he said.

'We'd better follow,' said Florence, getting down on her hands and knees and crawling into the tunnel.

'After you, rabbit,' said Dougal.

'Thank you,' said Dylan.

'I don't think I'm going to be able to manage it,' said Ermintrude.

'We'll send you some out,' said Dougal, crawling in.

'Hay flavour, if they have it,' called Ermintrude after him.

Inside it was quite light and cool, and surprisingly big. Brian and Florence were sitting on stools licking ice-creams.

'Hey, it's great!' said Brian.

Dougal and Dylan looked around.

There were lots of little tables and a long
low counter with tubs of ice-cream on it.
Behind the counter was a large lady.

'What's yours, boys?' she drawled.

'Er . . . tutti-frutti, mam,' said Dylan.

She looked at Dougal.

'You don't have tea, by any chance?' he said.

'TEA!!?' said the lady. 'TEA!!!?'

'It doesn't matter,' said Dougal hastily, 'just
give me what he's having.'

And he pointed to Brian.

The lady passed over a dish. Dougal took a
big lick.

'Errgh!' he said.

'Carrot flavour,' said Brian, happily. 'Can't
beat it.'

'Errgh!' said Dougal again.

'Something wrong, Mac?' said the lady, dangerously.

'Oh no . . . er no! Delicious,' said Dougal, and he took another little lick.

'That's typical of *you*,' he hissed at Brian.

'I can always be relied on,' said Brian, beaming.

There was a grunting noise from the tunnel and a huge man with a white beard came in.

'Evenin', Jane,' he said. 'Usual, please.'

Jane passed him over a dish of ice-cream.

'How's business?' she said.

'Oh, so-so,' said the man, 'just coming up to the rush. Always the same around Christmas.'

He threw back his coat and they saw that underneath he was dressed entirely in red.

'Hey!' said Dougal.

'Aren't you . . . ?'

'Hush, Dougal!'

said

Florence, quickly.

The man turned to Dougal.

'Were you addressing me?' he said.

'Er . . . no,' said Dougal.

The man finished his ice-cream, buttoned up his coat and left.

'Hey,' whispered Dougal, 'that was . . .'

'I *know*,' said Florence. 'Come along.'

They finished their ice-creams, said thank you to the lady and crawled outside again.

Ermintrude was standing with a dreamy look on her face.

'I've seen him!' she sighed. 'Oh, I've *seen* him!'

'Who?' said Dougal.

'*Him*!' said Ermintrude. 'Look!'

And away in the distance they saw another huge sledge drawn by six reindeer disappearing into the distance.

'I knew it was him!' said Dougal. 'Why wouldn't you let me ask him?'

'I don't think Father Christmas likes to be disturbed when he's working,' said Florence.

'That's not what they told me at Harrods,' said Brian.

'The North Pole is different,' said Florence. 'Come along.'

And they all got on the sledge and went back to the carpet.

'Had a good time?' said George.

'Marvellous,' said Florence. 'We've seen all sorts of things.'

'And all sorts of *people*,' said Ermintrude, dreamily. 'I wonder if he'll remember me?'

'We planted a flag at the North Pole,' said Brian.

'Flag?' said George. 'Union Jack?'

'Not *exactly*,' said Ermintrude, as they got on the carpet and rose into the air.

They flew out over the ice. Travelling in the same direction was the man on his big sledge drawn by six reindeer. George went past him.

'Busy?' he called.

'Will be come Christmas,' called the man, and they heard him booming with laughter as they flew on southwards.

America

Dougal woke up with a yawn and looked around. He gave a start.

'I don't believe it,' he whispered. 'Look!'

Florence, Ermintrude and Brian looked.

It was Dylan. He was awake and standing up.

'He's awake!' said Ermintrude.

'And standing up,' said Brian.

'Awake *and* standing up,' said Dougal. 'Must be the first time for *days*!'

They all went closer to Dylan. He was standing looking out over a huge prairie. They had landed right in the middle of it, and for miles and miles there was nothing but waving grass.

'Wow!' Dylan was murmuring. 'Wow! Wow! Wow!'

They all looked out and around.

'I don't see anything to "Wow!" about,' said Dougal. 'Where are we?'

'America,' said George. 'Texas, I think.'

'Don't you *know*?!' demanded Dougal.

'Not for certain,' said George, 'but see that sign? There'll be a stage-coach along soon and we can ask.'

They looked at the sign. It read . . .
BURLAP & CO
STAGING POST

'Oh, I've always wanted to go in a stage-coach,' breathed Florence.

'Well, better have some breakfast first,' said George.

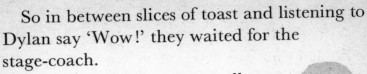

So in between slices of toast and listening to Dylan say 'Wow!' they waited for the stage-coach.

'Aren't we having a marvellous time?' sighed Florence.

'Lovely,' said Ermintrude. 'Absolutely lovely.'

They had just finished breakfast when the stage-coach arrived. It was drawn by six bony horses and driven by a man with a big black moustache. He was perched high up on a driving seat holding what looked like several dozen leather reins in his huge hands. Written across the side of the stage-coach were the words:

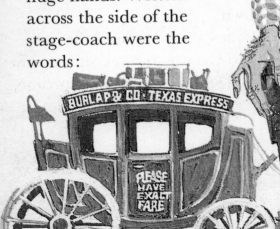

BURLAP & CO. TEXAS EXPRESS

PLEASE HAVE EXACT FARE

'Wow!' said Dylan.

As the horses panted and champed and jingled their harness, the driver got down stiffly and came over to them.

'How do you do?' he said.

'Er . . . tea?' said Dougal.

The driver looked at him.

'Two lumps, please,' he said.

Dougal poured a cup – the driver took it and sipped, his little finger crooked delicately.

'I take it you're all coming?' he said.

'Oh, yes please,' said Florence.

'Where to?' squeaked Brian.

'There's only one place to go around here,' said the driver, 'and that's Drybone.'

'Sounds *lovely*,' said Ermintrude, doubtfully.

George said he'd be waiting for them when they got back, and they all climbed into the coach and sat down.

The driver cracked the reins, and they all waved good-bye to George and set off at a trot across the prairie. Dougal, Brian, Ermintrude,

Dylan and Florence bumped about inside hanging on to little leather straps.

'A *real* stage-coach,' said Florence.

'Enjoying it?' shouted Brian.

'Immensely,' said Dougal, hanging on.

They hit a bump and Dougal was bounced up to the roof and down again.

'Immensely,' he said, grimly.

There was a 'whoop!' from behind.

'What's that?' said Florence.

Another 'whoop!'

Ermintrude stuck her head out of the window.

'What is it?' said Florence.

'I can't see anything,' said Ermintrude.

She looked up at the driver.

'What's that whooping, dear heart?' she said.

'Whooping?' said the driver, going quite pale. 'Did you say whooping?'

'That's what it sounded like,' said Ermintrude.

'INDIANS!!' shouted the driver, and he cracked his whip like anything. The coach shot forward very fast, and Ermintrude bounced back inside and landed on Dougal.

'He says it's Indians,' she said.

'It'll be a blessed relief,' said Dougal.

'Oh, sorry, dear dog,' said Ermintrude, getting off.

'Indians,' said Florence. 'How lovely.'

'But they fire bows and arrows at one,' squeaked Brian, nervously.

'Just the arrows, I think,' said Ermintrude.

'Well, that's *enough*!' said Brian. 'Especially if they *scalp* you too.'

'*Scalp*?' said Florence.

'Cutting all your hair off,' explained Brian. Dougal paled.

'What?' he said.

'They're going to have a lovely time with *you*,' said Brian.

'Oh, shut up,' said Dougal.

The 'whoops' got nearer. Florence peeked out of one of the windows. The stage-coach was going very swiftly, but following and catching up fast were the Indians.

'See them?' said Dougal.

'Yes,' said Florence.

'What do they look like?' said Brian.

'Very fierce,' said Florence.

'Oh my!' groaned Dougal.

The Indians caught up with the stage-coach and rode alongside whooping and shouting.

'Wow!' said Dylan.

The driver pulled the coach to a halt, and

the Indians drove round and round it in a circle making a great deal of noise.

'All right! All right! All right!' shouted the driver. 'We surrender!!'

'What do you mean, *we*?' screeched Dougal. '*I* don't surrender.'

'Oh, you're so brave!' said Brian.

'Are you surrendering?' demanded Dougal.

'Yes,' said Brian.

'Coward,' said Dougal.

'I know,' said Brian.

One of the Indians opened the door, and they all got out and stood in a little group. The Indians prodded them and one of them pulled at Dougal's hair.

'Don't you *dare*!' shouted Dougal.

The Indians gave a great shout and started to dance round Dougal, waving their bows and arrows.

The driver got down and came across to the others.

'They seem to have taken to my chum,' said Brian.

'Yes, I was afraid they would,' said the driver.

'Afraid?' said Florence.

'They've chosen him to be our champion,' said the driver. 'They'll have a contest. If your friend wins they'll let us go, if not . . .'

He paused.

'Yes?' said Brian.

'I'd rather not talk about it,' said the driver.

'What do you mean?' said Florence, aghast.

'You'll see,' said the driver.

Dougal came across to them carrying a bow and arrow.

'It's all right,' he said, airily. 'They just want to play games. They've invited me to have a little contest, so I suppose I'd better indulge them.'

'But, Dougal . . .' said Florence.

'Sh!!' whispered the driver. 'Better not tell him.'

'Tell him *what*?' said Florence.

'You'll see,' said the driver.

The Indians came over and pointed to a rock some way away. One of them took a bow and shot an arrow into the ground quite close to it. Then they pointed to Dougal.

'My turn?' said Dougal, laughing. 'Certainly!'

'Have you ever fired one of those bow and arrow things?' said Brian.

'No,' said Dougal, 'but I've read all about Robin Hood. He was British, you know.'

'Yes, I know,' said Brian, 'and he was also a dab hand with the old bow and arrow.'

'Oh, stop niggling,' said Dougal. 'I shall need your help.'

'Not likely,' said Brian.

'Snail!' said Dougal, sternly. 'Come here at once.'

'Under protest,' said Brian.

Dougal fastened the bow across Brian's horns, put an arrow in the string and pulled backwards with his teeth.

There was a twang and Brian somersaulted over Dougal's head and landed some way away.

'Oh really!' said Dougal. 'Really!! Can't you hold still?'

'I'm only little,' said Brian.

'Oh, don't be so pathetic,' said Dougal.

He fastened the bow and arrow again.

'Dig your heels in,' he said.

'I haven't got any heels,' shouted Brian.

'Well, dig *something* in,' said Dougal. 'Ready?'

'I suppose so,' sighed Brian.

Dougal pulled the bowstring again.

'I'm slipping!' screeched Brian.

'Hold on, Brian!' shouted Florence.

Dougal pulled some more. Brian started to slip backwards. Dougal pulled harder. Brian slipped further, and they both started to move backwards quite fast.

Dougal let go. The arrow went straight up in the air, and Brian shot towards the rock and landed on top of it with a shout. The arrow came down, hit the bowstring, shot forward and stabbed through the middle of Brian's hat.

'I say!' said Ermintrude.

The Indians gave a great shout and clustered round Dougal.

'We win, I think,' he said modestly, and was about to get back in the coach when the Indians dragged him away again.

'We make you chief,' they shouted.

'I say!' said Ermintrude.

Dougal was presented with a huge feathered head-dress and a tomahawk. He looked very imposing.

'Chief Shaggy-breeks,' whispered Brian.

'We'll have less of *that*,' said Dougal, 'unless you want to find yourself *hairless*.'

'I'm already hairless,' said Brian.

'I'll think of something,' said Dougal.

'What *are* you going to call yourself?' said Florence.

'I think Chief Greatest-Dog-that-Ever-Lived would be quite suitable,' said Dougal, modestly.

'Wow!' said Dylan.

They all got back in the coach and the Indians escorted them to the town of Drybone shouting a lot all the way.

'Noisy little bunch, aren't they?' said Brian.

'Choose your words, snail,' said Dougal. 'We Indians are very sensitive.'

In the town they all had something to eat and then went for a look around. There wasn't much to see as the town wasn't very big, so they walked up and down the main street so that everyone could see Dougal in his head-dress. Not that there were many people about. For some reason as soon as Dougal appeared everyone went indoors.

Except one man. He was very big with a large moustache and a big hat, and what seemed like an awful lot of guns hanging about his person. He stepped into the street in front of Dougal.

'Hold it right there,' he said.

'Hold what?' said Dougal.

'You an Indian?' asked the man.

'Yes, he is!' said Brian. 'That's Chief Grated Dog.'

'*Greatest* Dog,' corrected Dougal.

'Oh, sorry,' said Brian.

The man narrowed his eyes and gazed at Dougal.

'I don't like Indians,' he said, slowly.

'Well, that's not our fault,' said Brian. 'What do you want us to do about it?'

'Fight,' said the man.

'Fight?' said Dougal, aghast.

'You'd better be careful,' said Brian to the man. 'My friend is very fierce.'

'Shut up!' said Dougal, fiercely.

'You see!?' said Brian. 'Very fierce.'

'Then he won't mind fighting,' said the man, 'because I don't like Indians.'

'Oh, don't keep saying that,' said Dougal, sharply.

The man leapt back and crouched.

'Draw!' he snarled.

'Oh, he can't draw for toffee,' said Brian. 'He's just fierce.'

'Draw!' said the man again.

'You do meet some funny people,' muttered Dougal, starting to walk away.

There was a loud bang. Dougal and Brian jumped.

'Where are you going?' drawled the man, holding a gun which was smoking slightly.

'Er . . . we were thinking of having tea,' said Dougal.

'With cake,' squeaked Brian.

'You'll fight first,' said the man.

'We certainly will *not*,' said Dougal. 'We don't approve of fighting.'

'So don't rouse us,' said Brian, 'if you know what's good for you.'

'There's no need to say things like that,' hissed Dougal.

But Brian ignored him.

'My friend is a wizard with the bow and arrow,' he said, 'so be careful if you don't want to find yourself *punctured*.'

'What's he like with a gun?' said the man.

'Great!' said Brian. 'He's the greatest. He can shoot a potato at a hundred yards. Chipped,' he added.

The man looked impressed. He handed a revolver to Dougal.

'Show me,' he said.

'Now look what you've done,' said Dougal.

'What am I supposed to do with this?'

'Shoot a potato at a hundred yards,' said Brian.

'Have you *got* a potato?' said Dougal.

'No,' said Brian.

The man hadn't either. It wasn't something he normally carried apparently.

'Wait!' said Brian, dramatically.

He rushed off down the street.

'Where's he gone?' said the man.

'How should I know?' said Dougal. 'You started all this, remember?'

'There's no need to get tetchy,' said the man.

There was a shout from Brian. He was a long way away down the street and holding something on top of his hat.

'FIRE!' he shouted.

'What?!' shouted Dougal.

'FIRE!!!' screamed Brian.

Dougal held the big revolver in his mouth.

'The things I *do*,' he thought, and he closed his eyes and pulled the trigger.

There was a loud bang and Dougal fell over. Brian came scampering back in triumph. He was holding a potato. There was a hole right through the middle of it.

The man went quite white.

'Er . . . excuse me, stranger . . . er . . .
Big Chief,' he said. 'I . . . er . . . didn't mean
. . . er . . .'

He backed away and started to run.

'I don't think he'll bother us any more,'
said Dougal, airily.

He looked at the potato.

'Where did you find that?' he said.

'Lying around,' said Brian.

'Oh,' said Dougal.

'I made the hole with a stick,' said Brian.

'Oh,' said Dougal.

'I didn't want to take the chance that you
might miss,' said Brian. 'I hope you don't
mind?'

'No,' said Dougal.

They collected the others and caught the
stage-coach back to George and the flying
carpet.

'Where are we going now?' asked Florence.

'Secret,' said George. 'On you get and close
your eyes.'

They all got on and closed their eyes. With
a 'whoosh' the carpet took off, flew very fast
for a little while and then landed again.

'You can open them now,' said George.

They opened them and looked around.

'Where's this?' whispered Florence.

'Yes, where?' said Ermintrude.

'What a crazy place,' said Dylan.

'I think it's Mars,' said Brian.

'It's not Mars, it's home!' shouted Florence.

There was a 'boing' and Zebedee appeared.

'Welcome back,' he said. 'Have a good time?'

Everyone started to laugh. Mr Rusty and Mr MacHenry appeared, carrying a large table between them. On it was a huge tea, with a cake saying WELCOME BACK in pink icing.

'Isn't it funny we didn't recognise it?' said Florence.

'It's because you expected it to be somewhere else,' explained Zebedee. 'It's nice to have you back.'

'It's nice to *be* back,' they said.

'Where shall we go next time?' said Brian.

'We can recommend Bournemouth,' said Mr Rusty.

Dougal took a sip of tea and a mouthful of cake.

'We'll consider it,' he said, happily.